A BELL FOR URSLI

A PICTURE BOOK FROM THE ENGADINE

WRITTEN BY SELINA CHÖNZ
ILLUSTRATED BY ALOIS CARIGIET

orell füssli Verlag AG

15th edition 2012

ISBN 978-3-280-01483-7

AN EXPLANATION

All through the summer in the Engadine Mountains of Switzerland the cattle feed in the mountain meadows, carrying bells round their necks. The calves have little bells and the cows have big ones. When they come into their sheds for the winter the bells are taken off. In March when winter is over, the Spring Festival comes, and the bells are rung in the village to celebrate the end of the cold, dark days. All the boys march in procession through the street, each one carrying the biggest bell he can, and they ring their bells to drive the winter away and welcome back the sunny spring. And the village people smile, and fill the bells with cakes and nuts and apples. But only the big boys can carry the big bells: the little boys come at the tail of the procession carrying little calf-bells. This is the story of Ursli, and of the adventure he has when the Spring Festival comes round and he decides that he is old enough to have a big bell for the first time.

High in the mountains, far and blue,
There lives a small boy just like you.
See the wee village, poor but neat?
His is the last house in the street.

The house is old and snug and small,
With pictures painted on the wall.
Look closer. Do you see those two
Standing there dressed in red and blue?
A man and wife, with one small son.
His name is Ursli. See him run!

Yes, here our mountain boy you see,
Quite like a man, you must agree.
Upon his head a pointed hat,
(The mountain, too, is shaped like that.)
It's made of soft wool from the sheep
That now in Ursli's stable sleep.
For Ursli's mother spins, weaves, stitches,
And knits his shirt and hat and breeches.
His father has the boots to make,
And toils all day for Ursli's sake.

But Ursli helps his father, too,
As much as any man would do,
Waters the cows and brings them hay,
Cleans out the stalls by break of day.
When mother calls him to the house
Ursli comes scurrying like a mouse
To bring the yoke with water pails,
Or help to cook. He never fails
To milk his friend the goat, and see
The milk froth white as white can be.

When he's done everything he's able
In house and yard, in shed and stable,
He rushes out with cheerful noise
To play with all the village boys.
Today he tells them he must borrow
A bell that he can ring tomorrow
In the Procession of the Bells.
See how with pride young Ursli swells!
He thinks he'll get one large and loud,
And help the big boys lead the crowd.

At Uncle Gian's farmhouse, all
The boys for bells have come to call.
Good uncle quickly brings them out,
And everyone begins to shout:
"The big one's mine!" "I want the best!"
Ursli is pushed behind the rest.
And when at last the front he gains
The tiniest tinkle-bell remains.
Now he sheds sad and bitter tears,
He'll be a laughing stock, he fears,
The boys already laugh and boo:
"Tinkle-bell Ursli, look at you!
When the Procession marches past,
Tinkle-bell Ursli, you'll be last!"

The boys go off. They all despise him.
Poor Ursli's bell quite horrifies him.
He'd hoped to march in front this year,
Not with the small boys in the rear.
In front the fine young men march proudly,
Swinging their bells and singing loudly.
They lead the way, with clang and yell,
Past every stable, every well.
In every house they march about
Ringing to drive the winter out,
And then with all their might they sing
To welcome back the happy spring.
Then everybody's glad and thrilled,
With nuts and cakes the bells are filled.
But outside, in the crisp, cold snow,
The little boys must wait, you know;
With little calf-bells back they come,
And bring their empty pockets home.
Ursli no calf intends to be.
Tinkle-bell Ursli? No, not he!

He's ready to do anything,
But all ideas have taken wing.
He thinks and thinks, then gives a hop —
Their summer hut on the mountain top!
There on a nail there used to hang
As big a bell as ever rang!

As quick as thought he's on his way,
No fears would make our Ursli stay.
He braves dark forests, footpaths steep,
The narrow bridge, the chasm deep.

But soon his burst of joy is done.
As he climbs higher, near the sun,
The snow is melting. In he sinks
Above his knees. Poor Ursli thinks
He's going to cry. But who will hear?
No crying will bring Mother near.
Perhaps the great bell, after all,
No longer hangs upon the wall —
"If it's not there", he thinks in sorrow,
"Whatever should I do tomorrow?"
But forward go his steps again,
And now, the hut grows near and plain,
Glowing beneath the sunset light
As Ursli sees it come in sight.

The hard climb's done, he's here at last.
But now he finds the door shut fast,
Nor will his shaking move the thing.
The key is kept on Father's ring!
Still, there's the window. Ursli's thin.
He can just manage to squeeze in.

The nail's still there. And on it, yes,
The great bell hangs, as we can guess.
"Tinkle-bell Ursli!" See him grin.
"Oh, how they'll stare when I walk in!"
He's scrambled on the bed, and stretched
High up the wall — and down it's fetched.
Heavy and round, how fine to see!
A belt of flowered embroidery
To hang it from, with clasp of gold.
And how it rings! So clear and bold!

By now he's hungry as can be,
He looks all round, what can he see?
Ah! Hanging up above the dishes,
A loaf, the very thing he wishes.
Then he sits down. It's grand to eat.
But he's tired out, from head to feet,
And since he's free from every care
Slumber comes softly, light as air.
The bed of straw's a cosy nest.
In deep, sound sleep can Ursli rest.

Now in the valley, far below,
To house and stable homeward go
Tired men and beasts, to dream at ease.
But underneath the mountain trees
Small fox and chamois, deer and hare,
Out in the snow must coldly fare.
There in the moonlight they can trace
Child footprints on the earth's white face.
And up the snow track softly creeping
They reach the hut and Ursli sleeping.
Fox pricks his ears, and says to deer:
"What can that boy be doing here?"

Mother is waiting. Darkness reigns.
Small stars shine through the window panes.
She looks all round in street and square
To see if Ursli's hiding there,
While Father by the stove sits down
And asks quite crossly for his son.
But though at every house they call,
No one has seen the boy at all.
Now everybody seeks all over,
But still no Ursli they discover.
In vain the lantern lights the gloom,
Its beams do not bring Ursli home.

His anxious parents, worn and sad,
Go home again without their lad.
They sit and watch the pine-logs burn,
And still their boy does not return.
Poor mother weeps. The clock ticks on.
Alas, where has young Ursli gone?
Father can't settle anyhow;
He starts to carve his son a cow.
The village sleeps, but wide awake
They sit and wait for day to break.

Now swiftly flies the deep, dark night.
The mountain sees the sun's first light.
And as the sunny morning breaks
Young Ursli rubs his eyes and wakes.
He must at once be on his way —
Whatever will his parents say?
He takes the bell. Quick, see him go
Running across the firm, hard snow,
For overnight it froze again
On mountain, pasture, wood and plain.
The animals flee far and wide
So swift is Ursli's homeward stride.

A twinkling, and, as you can see,
Before his own carved door stands he.
Three times he bangs the knocker down,
And footsteps to the door have flown.

Quick at the latch his mother tugs,
Her darling son she sees and hugs,
While Ursli climbs her skirt and clings,
Arms and bell round her neck he flings.

The Bell Procession's on its way,
And who is that in front? Hurray!
It's little Ursli, ding, dong, dell,
Who has by far the biggest bell.
And everyone is full of joy
To see once more that little boy.

To dinner now the three sit down,
Vanished is every care and frown,
And Ursli, his adventure past,
Tells all that happened, first to last,
And how he has escaped from shame.
Father's too overjoyed to blame.
Mother brings chestnuts, piping hot,
With cream poured over – such a lot!
And while they watch him happily,
Young Ursli eats enough for three.

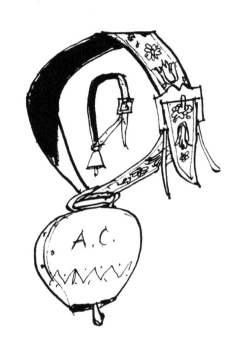